PHOENIX CHILD

A MODERN MYTH
SHORT STORY

ALEXANDRIA BLAELOCK

BlueMere Books

MELBOURNE, AUSTRALIA

Ordering Information:
Discounts are available on quantity purchases. For details, contact orders@bluemerebooks.com.

Phoenix Child/Alexandria Blaelock
paperback ISBN: 978-1-925749-08-3
digital ISBN: 978-1-925749-09-0

Book Layout © BookDesignTemplates.com

PHOENIX CHILD

The day Aidan found Aisling's grave was bright, sunny and lightly scented with Spring Blossom.

His long black coat soaked up the sunshine, but barely warmed his frozen heart.

That it was the right kind of beautiful day for a picnic seemed like the most hideous kind of prank a deity could play.

Better that it was as dark and stormy as his mood.

The scrap of land her bones lay beneath was unloved, with deeply rooted sunny dandelions dipping their heads in the light breeze.

While she had no monument, someone had laid a rudimentary marker.

It broke his heart - this was so different from the future he'd dared to imagine for her.

The roses hung from his limp hands, and his sulphurous tears sizzled as they hit the ground.

He sighed and tried not to think of her brightness; her glowing red hair and chiming ready laugh.

She'd been the epitome of a lively Irish girl.

《《 • 》》

Her zest for life had kept his attention.

As if she'd no moment to lose, she dove headfirst into everything she did.

No second thoughts or guessing allowed.

Including love with him. Poor dear Aisling. She'd warmed him to his cold empty core.

He shivered and pulled his coat tighter around his body. When you're born from fire, you're always cold without it.

That's how he'd met her the first time. Up a mountain bathing in fire. She'd seen his wings and thought he was an angel.

Perhaps that was why she'd thought he was safe and didn't run away screaming like most humans. Mind you, she was only something like five years old at the time.

Too young to be afraid of much.

"Are you here to take me to heaven?"

"Now, why would I do that?"

"I thought maybe my ma had asked for me to visit. She's not been gone long, and I'm sure she misses me as much as I miss her."

She sat heavily on a rock, contorting her little face in an effort not to cry.

Despite the fire of their birth, his people were dispassionate, so maybe it was just curiosity that made him step from the fire and crouch to look at her face.

He brushed a smear of dirt from her soft pale cheek.

"I'm sure your mother misses you too, but you'll be together soon enough. Dry your eyes and go home to your family."

He placed his palm on the top of her head and gifted her strength in sorrow.

He couldn't see the future clearly but felt she'd need it. Humans always do.

《《 • 》》

The second time he'd met Aisling, he'd felt an odd compulsion to return to the mountain.

Maybe it was the fresh rowan scented air, closer access to the sun or maybe he felt her calling him.

As he flew in, there she was, delightfully slim young teen hands on hips, foot tapping, as if she'd been waiting.

And he was very late.

"Ah, it's yourself again is it?"

He folded his wings and took a moment to look at her. "I see you're growing up strong and straight."

"No thanks to you; I've been praying and praying for you to come back."

Aidan smiled, her audacity delighted, surprised and intrigued him. "And what is it that you're asking then?"

"Well," she drew a circle on the ground with a toe, "I've been missing my ma. I wondered if she is ok and has any advice about Killian for me."

"I haven't seen her for a while, but I'm sure she's fine."

God help him, he couldn't help but wish death upon this unknown but vexing boy Killian. "What's the problem with this Killian?"

He wasn't really listening to what she said, just enjoying the sparkling lilt of her voice, her bright green eyes and messy bun.

The way the white blouse of her school uniform brightened her face and the remains of a scab on her knee.

The warmth of her body and animated gestures sent him the pure, innocent scent of bath soap.

Eventually, she ran out of words, and he reached out to tuck a stray lock of hair behind her ear.

"I know this won't be what you want to hear, but you should put this Killian out of your thoughts.

"Focus on your schoolwork, work hard to get into a good University and earn yourself a brighter future than you can get here with him."

While she pouted at his answer, she wasn't upset by it.

It seemed she was more or less expecting it, and he guessed this was the right kind of angelic advice.

He almost laughed at the absurdity of being confused with one, but how could she know any different?

"What is your name child?"

"Aisling. What's yours?"

Up until that point, he hadn't needed one, so he plucked one from her head, "Well Aisling, my name is Aiden. I'm pleased to meet you."

They shook hands before Aisling giggled and fled.

《《 • 》》

Aiden had been fighting his way to the bar when he saw Aisling the third time.

Third time lucky, they say, but he couldn't tell if it was her or him who was the lucky one.

She'd been on his mind for a time, which was why he was in the pub in the first place. But somehow, it'd slipped his mind he was in a University town on a Friday night.

She was breathtaking.

Fully absorbed, dancing joyfully like a goddess. Her whole body moving lightly and gracefully, bouncing perfectly in time with the music.

She'd bobbed her hair in the meantime, and it seemed to be dancing along of its own volition.

A spotlight lit her up, and as his mouth fell open, it seemed the deafening roar of rock music suddenly fell silent.

He'd always felt a species that reproduced itself by dying was doomed.

What set of circumstances leads evolution down the path of procreative self-immolation?

Perhaps it was just an extreme version of his people's tradition of noble self-sacrifice.

And maybe that's why he was the last of his kind - he'd never felt deeply enough about anyone to consider sacrificing himself for them.

She glowed like fate. As she turned, her eyes met his, and a smile lit up her face.

Before he could move, she was before him, looking up into his face.

He bent down to hear her speak, and she kissed him on the lips.

"Aiden, here you are at last," her beery breath caressing his cheek.

It was too late to run, and in any case, he had nowhere to run to.

Her luminous delight at seeing him held him transfixed - no one had ever been so delighted to see him.

He had no option but to follow her and see where she took him.

No matter the cost.

《《 • 》》

The day he'd lost her had started ordinarily enough.

Looking back, he couldn't help feeling he should've known it would be the last day.

Human lives are so short, and so easily extinguished. But he'd been so deep in the joy of just being with her he'd barely given the end of hers any thought.

The morning was so precious he could hardly bear to remember it.

They'd made love between crisp, clean sheets. The smell of her enveloped him, the taste of her lingered on his lips, and her soft cries echoed in his ears.

He'd been so happy.

She'd kissed the top of his head as she handed him coffee and a bacon butty.

Then whispered she had a secret to share later. No amount of kissing or tickling had prized it from her lips.

Now he'd never know.

He'd been driving her to work in her little excuse for a car when it happened.

She'd been singing along with the radio, and he'd glanced at her for just an instant, but it was too long.

A truck veered across the road and hit the car head-on. He'd just enough time to teleport her to safety before he was engulfed by the flames.

≪≪ • ≫≫

He'd been shocked and surprised to wake up.

As the flames took him, he'd thought his life was over, and at that moment was comforted by the belief that she would survive.

He'd finally found someone worthy of sacrificing himself for, and his long life had come to an end.

How could it be that it continued?

As soon as he'd been strong enough, he'd started looking for her.

It had taken several years to find out she was dead.

It was hard to deal with. But he was buoyed by the thought of finding her new incarnation and winning her heart again.

He'd searched for her across countries and continents. Year after year, he fruitlessly crisscrossed the globe every time he thought he'd heard the bright spark of her soul.

But she simply wasn't there.

Perhaps her firm belief in one life, followed by an eternal heavenly afterlife had prevented her rebirth.

He hoped she was happy in her heaven, but it was so hard to know they would never be together again.

More years had passed as he'd searched for her final resting place, and now here he was, standing before it.

Disregarding the condition of his black dress pants, he knelt at the foot of her grave and tenderly laid the roses down.

This is where he would end himself. If he couldn't be with her, he didn't want to be at all.

Bowing his head and allowing his tears to flow freely, he thought about how little impact he'd made during his life.

With Aisling gone, there was no one left to remember him.

He absently uprooted a dandelion and laid it aside. Pulling up another, he wondered if he was the most pathetic of all god's creatures.

He'd just skipped across the surface of other people's lives like a mayfly. At best barely noticed, at worst, a momentary nuisance.

He was so engrossed in his thoughts; he didn't notice the young man until he spoke.

"Did you know the woman in this grave?"

Aiden, startled, looked up.

The man was tall and well-formed. His green eyes were sympathetic and curious in his luminous face.

He held out a hand, and Aiden took it to help pull himself up.

He pulled a handkerchief from his coat pocket and wiped his eyes.

"We were close for a time when we were younger."

"My mother died when I was a child, so I don't know too much about her. I'd love to buy you a drink and hear your story if you've time."

"What happened to your father and her family?"

"He died in a car crash before I was born, and her family threw her out. We don't keep in touch."

"I'm so sorry to hear that. My poor Aisling deserved better. And poor you with no family."

"Ah well," the young man ran his fingers through his close-cropped hair in a way that looked vaguely familiar "you don't miss what you never had."

He held his arm out to point the way, "My name's Aiden by the way, what's yours?"

THE END

ABOUT THE AUTHOR

Alexandria Blaelock writes stories, some of them for *Ellery Queen's Mystery Magazine* and *Pulphouse Fiction Magazine*. She's also written four self-help books applying business techniques to personal matters like getting dressed, cleaning house, and feeding your friends.

As a recovering Project Manager, she's probably too fond of sticking to plan. She lives in a forest because she enjoys birdsong, the scent of gum leaves and the sun on her face. When not telecommuting to parallel universes from her Melbourne based imagination, she watches K-dramas, talks to animals, and drinks Campari. At the same time.

Discover more at www.alexandriablaelock.com.

BOOKS BY ALEXANDRIA BLAELOCK

Stress Free Dinner Parties
Build Your Signature Wardrobe
Holistic Personal Finance
Ms Blaelock's Book of Minimally Viable
Housekeeping

www.ingramcontent.com/pod-product-compliance
Lightning Source LLC
Chambersburg PA
CBHW070456170726
48291CB00005B/1776